OMEGA, JE T'AIME

A VALE VALLEY VALENTINE ROMANCE

SUMMER CHASE

EVER HAPPY BOOKS

Omega, je t'aime

❀ Created with Vellum

ABOUT VALE VALLEY

SWEET, SMEXY, MPREG

When former Mayor Rosemary and her husband Trenton Vale, started Vale Valley, it was with the goal that all would be welcomed. The Vale's wanted their town to be a safe haven for all who was searching for a place to belong. Now with five thousand residents and counting, Vale Valley is filled with people and beings with diverse backgrounds. No other town is like Vale Valley where were-creatures, witches, ghosts, and many others can live in harmony. The residents of Vale Valley know about the many creatures in their little town and it makes them feel safe and protected.

Vale Valley a small but bustling town and have everything that a big city would have. The residents are able to feed and rejuvenate their souls. From their Health Center, to the local bar Club Incubus where the residents are entertained by a live band, Vale's General Hospital that specializes in male pregnancies, and let's not forget Vale Valley Inn and Restaurant or The Dozing Dragon's B&B. If there's something you're looking for Vale Valley will certainly provide fulfilling your every desire.

One of Vale Valley's many secrets is that it is only visible to those who need to find love and a home.

ONE

EDWIN

"DADDY, WHERE DO BABIES COME FROM?"

I frown down at my five-year-old son, unsure how to answer that. It's not that I'm a prude about telling him that—I can be up front with Colton, and he'd understand as well as a child can. No, it's more about the fact that this will bring up Greg, my late husband and Colton's omega-father who died in childbirth.

It's something you don't want to bring up when you're going out for donuts. I know that even if I start talking about it, Colton will make the connection.

Even thinking about Greg right now, my heart constricts tightly in my chest.

"Daddy?" Colton peers up at me, concern on his face. "You okay?"

I swallow thickly and nod. "Yep. It's just one of those adult things, and I'm not sure how to approach it."

"Oh." Colton knows very well what an *adult thing* could be and his boundaries with it. "We can talk about it later, Daddy?"

I nod. Five years later, a year later, next week...any of

them. Just so that I can have time on how to think about Greg and how to talk to Colton about it. Call me a wimp.

Some alpha I am.

"What kind of donut do you want?" I ask, not-so-subtly changing the subject.

Luckily, Colton doesn't catch onto the change, and his eyes light up at the thought. "Jelly-filled and sprinkles!"

Of course.

I chuckle. Colton thinks jelly-filled donuts are the best because my father loves those donuts, and he thinks that his grandfather is the bee's knees. The sprinkles are just because he loves a good sugary dask of sprinkles on anything.

"Jelly and sprinkles it is," I say, ruffling his hair. Yes, I'm a doting sap for my son, but how could I not be? He is such a character, and I'm so grateful to have him in my life.

We stop at a stoplight, waiting for the pedestrian cross-walk to signal it's all right for us to go, and that's when I notice the man standing across the road. No, not just a man. A hot omega in a business casual suit, with a tie and a messenger bag. He looks to be about my age, put-together, and with stylish haircut. I find myself looking at him, curious, and admittedly a bit turned on.

As if feeling the weight of my eyes on him, the omega turns toward us, and our eyes meet. Even from across the street, I can tell that they're hazel. Damn, I have a thing for hazel eyes.

Unusual. Beautiful. Striking.

And I feel my cock stand straight to attention. He has a mind of his own, and I shift uncomfortably to make standing less uncomfortable. The edges of the omega's lips lift up in a smile, like he knows my physical response to him.

Damn. His smile is sexy.

"Daddy," Colton says, interrupting my dirty thoughts, "the sign says go."

I swallow thickly and nod. "Right. Let's go."

That means we'll have to walk right by the omega, since it seems like he's crossing the street too. Don't mind if I do. Maybe I can delay Colton's donuts long enough to get the omega's name. Or phone number. Or kiss him.

We start walking, and the omega does as well. I feel my heart pounding in my chest, and I hold my breath, waiting for that exact moment to catch his scent, and get a sense of who he is as a person.

Things never work out the way we plan, though.

Nearly halfway across the crosswalk, Colton's body suddenly goes limp, and he collapses to the ground. I was so enamored by the omega, that I almost don't catch him before his head hits the pavement.

Thank my lucky stars I do catch him, though.

"Colton!" I screech, panic taking over me as I kneel next to him. Bit by bit, horror and helplessness overtake me. "Colton!"

My son doesn't respond. His eyes roll into the back of his head, and his body shakes uncontrollably. I notice as well that there's a growing wet spot on the front of his pants from him releasing his bladder.

A seizure? Epilepsy? I have no fucking clue, only that my son is unresponsive.

Unresponsive like Greg was.

I let out a wail. "Colton, answer me!" I can't help my shake of his shoulders, in case he's faking it. But there's no reason for him to, and Colton doesn't do that kind of thing.

What the hell is happening?

"*Arrêt!*"

I'm confused as I look up to see the omega standing in front of Colton and me. In a daze, I realize that he's holding his arms up and waving his hands to stop…

"Fuck!" I shout as the bus stops and narrowly avoids hitting us. I'd been so absorbed in Colton's state that I didn't even consider the traffic once the light turned green. The omega—who I just realize shouted *stop* in French—saved our lives.

And it doesn't stop there.

"I'm a doctor," he says in a thick accent as he kneels next to us. "What happened?"

"I—I don't know," I stammer. I'm nearly tearing my hair out with worry. "We were just crossing the road to get some donuts, when he collapsed, and, and, and—"

"Let's get him out of the road," the omega says gruffly as he lifts Colton in his arms. "Vale Valley General is right around the corner, and I can help him."

I meet his eyes again. "You can help?"

"I'm a pediatrician," the omega says, all business once again. As if that answers everything. "I can take care of him."

I don't know who this man is, but he's already saved our lives once. I trust him implicitly.

So I nod.

———

"IT APPEARS that Colton suffered a generalized epileptic seizure," Dr. Marchand, the omega, tells me later. We're standing outside of Colton's room in the pediatric ICU, where my son is sleeping soundly. There's no longer a seizure, but after what happened earlier today, I don't want to take my eyes off him in case there's another one.

I swallow thickly. "What does that mean, exactly? Will he have more in the future like that?"

Because if that's a hint of things to come, I'm terrified.

"I am not certain," Dr. Marchand tells me, frowning. He follows my gaze to the window of Colton's room. "There are any number of reasons for epileptic episodes in children. And fifty to seventy-five percent of patients have complete seizure remission."

I gnaw on my bottom lip. "But if it doesn't? Are there any long-term effects of this?"

The omega gives me a comforting smile. "We'll have to run some tests to be certain," he says. "But I promise you that I will do everything in my power to take care of him."

Even though there are so many question marks and so many unknowns in my life from here on out, his words comfort me, and I nod slightly. "Thank you."

He smiles. "Just doing my job, Mr. Schneider."

Before I know what I'm doing, I wrap the omega up into a tight hug, and it's me who's shuddering with barely contained sobs.

"No, I'm serious," I tell him. "Thank you. Thank you so very much. You saved Colton's life twice today. First with stopping the buses and second with treating him so well. Not to mention, saving mine once as well." I pull back and look at him, the promise bubbling up in my throat. "If there's anything I can do in the future to help you out in any way, Dr. Marchand, I will do it. I am forever in your debt."

I realize how ridiculous that sounds as soon as it escapes my lips. It almost feels like I'm offering him something sketchy in return for what he did. Then again, if that's what it takes to make it up to him, that's certainly fine with me.

Dr. Marchand gave me my son back. And that means the whole world to me.

The omega smiles serenely at me. "Please," he says, "after a day like today, you can call me Jacques."

I love how his name leaves his lips and sounds so hot. I grin and stick my hand out.

"Pleased to meet you, Jacques. I'm Edwin."

He takes my hand and gives it a strong pump. "The pleasure's all mine. And I'm sure this is not the first time we'll be working with each other."

Little does he know, I'm one-hundred percent serious. And I'm going to figure out what I can do to show him how gracious I am for him saving my son's life.

TWO

JACQUES

USUALLY, the first thing anyone notices about me is the accent. Because no matter how many reruns of *Seinfeld* I watch, no matter how many times I practice sounding American, my thick accent gives me away.

"Oh my god, I love your accent!" the older woman on the bus coos at me, giving me a rosy-cheeked smile. "Where are you from?"

"Marseilles," I tell her, and she gives me a blank look, one that I get a lot. I really should just default to an easier one. "France."

"Ohhh," she says, sitting back. "I love France. I would love to go, but I haven't had the time or the money."

"I highly recommend it." I wink at her. "Although you live in Vale Valley, and it's just as pretty as some places in France." I'm not being facetious about that either. There are plenty of reasons why I choose to make Vale Valley my home, and it's not just because I work at the local doctor's practice here at the hospital.

"Yes," she says with a sigh. "I do love Vale Valley."

I glance out the window of the bus, and it's snowing a little outside, dusting the snow drifts that are already on the roads and sidewalks. It's early February, and there are plenty of picturesque spots in the town that make it homey and wonderful. Storefronts have their Valentine's decorations out, and there are posters advertising special meals and activities for couples in love.

It makes me wish I had an alpha to take me out. Almost. Even though I'm still young and take care of myself, I honestly think it's that French accent that turns men off from me.

Like they're intimidated by me.

Oh well. It probably means another Valentine's spent alone. I'll probably just cuddle up with my pug, Carlin, watch a few movies, and consider it done.

"How long have you lived here?" the woman asks, breaking through my thoughts.

I shrug, thinking about it, although I do have a fair idea of when I came here. "A little over four years ago." Having visa deadlines and expiration dates will do that to you, and my own visa application has been weighing heavily on my head as I have yet to hear back about it.

"Are you planning on staying here?"

Nosy, isn't she? But I smile and nod. "I do."

I look to the front of the bus as it slows to a stop. "This is me," I tell her as I get to my feet and grab my messenger bag. "*Bonne journée.*"

She laughs loudly as I step off the bus to Vale Valley General Hospital. Most of my professional time as a pediatrician has been at this hospital, and I can't imagine going anywhere else. This is my home, both personal and professional.

"Good morning, Dr. Marchand," the admin assistant, Marsha, says as I enter the pediatric ward. She sits behind the counter, sifting through files as she does so. "How are you doing today?" She smiles coyly at me.

"*Très bien*, and yourself?"

"*Spectaculaire*," she responds, and I let out a full-bellied laugh.

"You have been practicing," I tell her.

"Just for you," she says with a wink. "Here's your office mail," she adds, as she hands me a pile of envelopes. Tons of marketing materials for penis pills, I am sure. Never mind that I'm a pediatrician.

"Thank you, Marsha." I flip through it, curiously. I stop when I get to a large manila envelope with a federal seal on it.

My visa paperwork.

My stomach falls to my feet. I have been waiting for this paperwork for nearly a year now, as my H1-B visa is nearly expired. I applied for lawful permanent residency through a lawyer, making sure that all my paperwork was filed correctly.

I've heard some horror stories of what happens if even your fingerprints aren't in a good state.

"Thank you again, Marsha," I tell her, feeling as though I'm in a daze as I walk by her.

I'm sure she noticed the change in my demeanor, because she shouts behind me, "Let me know if there's anything I can do, Dr. Marchand!"

I step onto an elevator, feeling that flurry of butterflies from within me. I have to open it in my office. Maybe after

I meditate some, because I don't know if I can handle the stress or the pressure.

Dr. Loomis, an obstetrician at the hospital, steps into the elevator car behind me and gives me a once-over. "Everything okay?" he asks.

I nod and lick my lips. "I hope so. I have some important paperwork that arrived today, and I hope it's all fine."

He grins encouragingly. "I'm sure it will be."

I don't feel that way, though. I can barely contain my nerves as I get off at my floor and head to my office. I shut the door behind me, toss the envelopes on the desk, and open the blinds on the window.

Still a beautiful day outside. Nothing bad can happen on days like this, right?

I glance back at the pile and then go back to the desk and sit down. Screw it, I can't wait anymore. I grab the large piece, sit back in my chair, and open it.

My French passport tumbles onto the table, and I could look through there to see if there is a new sticker. But instead, I opt for the official-looking letter that accompanies it.

DEAR DR. JACQUES VINCENT MARCHAND,

Thank you for your application for a green card. However, we regret to inform you that...

I BLINK, feeling as if my gaze has gotten fuzzy. No. No, that's not right. There is no "regret to inform you" in a letter that is meant to say that I have received my green card and I can stay in Vale Valley indefinitely.

That is how it is supposed to go.

Only when I read it again, with a clear head, the message hasn't changed. In fact, it only gets worse.

The United States Citizenship and Immigration Services has not granted my visa because of an "error" in my application and a lapse in my visa status. Which doesn't make sense, because I've filed everything through my immigration lawyer on time and with plenty of evidence to back up every piece of information I supplied to the government.

I shouldn't have been turned down. I am one of the few pediatricians in Vale Valley and I specialize in brain disorders. There is a definite need for my skill set here, so I don't see why they turned me down.

Well, you thought this would happen, I tell myself. *You thought it could*

I am also a pessimist, and even though I had thought the worst could happen, I truly didn't think it would. Not until now when I'm seeing it in black and white.

Fuckfuckfuckfuck...

My lawyer!

My lawyer will know what to do. I fish out my cellular phone and dial John Wells, my immigration lawyer. Of course, it goes to voicemail. I pace around my office while the voice recording walks me through the various steps and numbers that I can call for immediate help.

For the amount of money I paid John, he better give me immediate help.

"Hey, John, this is Jacques Marchand," I say, and even to my own ears, my own accent twangs in my ears. "I just received a letter from the government stating that my green card has been denied. I—" My voice trails off, because I'm so upset, I know that I'll say something I regret and I need his help.

Hell, I need anyone's help.

"Call me back," I finish finally. Because I have nothing else to say.

I end the call and practically fling my phone across the room. I'm bottled up with energy, and I debate for a moment if I should run an internet search for any sort of help. But I've read those horror stories in the past. And my own horror story is coming to life.

No, looking up anything would just make me more anxious.

"*Bordel de merde,*" I mutter as I run my fingers through my hair. I need to figure out what to do with my hands, because I'm feeling so jittery from that information.

There's a knock at the door.

"*Oui?*" I ask.

It's Kim, one of the on-staff nurses.

"Dr. Marchand, your nine o'clock is here." She pauses in the doorway. "What's wrong?"

I have to act like I'm normal. I have to act like there's nothing wrong. I have to pretend that everything is all right. Until John calls me back, I can't do anything about it, and I have patients who need me.

They're part of the reason why I have to stay here.

I grin her. "I'm all right. Just give me a minute and I'll be there."

She frowns but doesn't pursue the matter. "All right." She closes the door behind her and leaves me alone with my thoughts.

I need to keep myself together. I take a deep sigh, rub my thighs with my hands, and stand.

It will be all right. I'll figure out a way of staying here. I just need to keep myself together.

THREE
EDWIN

"DADDY, WHY ARE YOU NERVOUS?" Colton swings his legs as he sits on the examination table. "Is it because Dr. Marchand is coming in?" He can't stop grinning.

Shit, my kid suspects my unrequited attraction to his pediatrician. Score one awkward point for Edwin Schneider, single alpha-father with a seven-year-old kid and a boner for his doctor. After that fateful day in the crosswalk, Jacques has been Colton's pediatrician to monitor any further seizures.

I was serious when I told him that I'd pay back the debt. I don't think Jacques believes me, though.

"Just want to make sure you're all right," I tell Colton with a tight-lipped smile. He hasn't had another epileptic seizure since then as well, to my absolute relief. But it's always in the back of my mind that he could fall again.

The worry of a father never ends.

"And it's not just because Dr. Marchand is hot-hot-hot?" Colton teases.

Great. I'm being trolled by a seven-year-old. "You're

not supposed to think about your doctor that way, Colton."
I cross my arms and give him a stern look.

"I don't think *you're* supposed to, either," he counters,
erupting into giggles.

"He saved your life," I remind him. "And I'm just
grateful for that. You should be, too."

"Uh-huh." His legs swing back and forth even more.
"Can I get a donut after this? From Lakelan's daddy's
place."

"If you're good." I raise an eyebrow. "And I'm not sure
what you are right now."

He pouts for a moment but doesn't say anything else as
the door to the room opens, and Jacques—*Dr. Marchand*, I
mean, because I've tried keeping that distance between us,
even though he told me to call him *Jacques*—is standing
there, looking dapper in his white coat. I've known him for
two years now, and he still never fails to steal my breath
away. He's always well put-together, well-trimmed, well-
mannered.

Except today. Today, I can see there's something wrong
in his eyes and on his face.

"Okay, Colton," he says as he rifles through some
papers in Colton's manila folder. He looks up, and I
notice that his eyes are bloodshot. "How are you feeling
today?"

Goddamn, his accent is sexier every time I hear it.

"Fine," Colton answers.

I'm grateful that he doesn't bring up what we were
talking about. I'd be mortified if Dr. Marchand knew
about my feelings for him.

Dr. Marchand sets the folder down and picks up an
otoscope. "Kim says that you came in here with an
earache?"

"Yeah, it's been getting worse and worse, and I figured it was time to bring him in," I say.

He lifts the otoscope and checks Colton's ears. "Just the right one, correct?"

"Correct," I say.

After a moment, Dr. Marchand steps back and gives Colton a bewildered look. "Well, no wonder it's hurting! You have an elephant in there!"

Colton's eyes are wide. "I do?"

"*Oui.*" Dr. Marchand glances at me. "His Etruscan tubes are filled with fluid, indicating an infection," he says in a serious voice. He inspects the rest of Colton, from his mouth to his chest and his reflexes. I watch him interact with my son, and even though I can tell that something is weighing heavily on his mind, he still treats Colton with respect and kindness.

Dr. Marchand has the best bedside manner of any doctor I've ever worked with.

"Well," he says at length. "The good news is that it appears to just be the one elephant in the ear. There's a little infection on the left side, but nothing that a round of antibiotics won't clear up." He pats Colton's knee. "You will be fine in a few days' time. We'll get that elephant out."

"And I shouldn't be worried about anything else?" I ask.

Dr. Marchand frowns with a slight shake of his head. "No, not really. Just make sure that he finishes the entire prescription."

I nod. "Thank you."

He writes something on a notepad, tears it off, and hands it to me. "That is your prescription," he explains

I pocket it. "Thank you."

And now, awkwardly, I wonder if I should ask if there's anything else I can do for him. Since he seems so distraught over something.

I gulp back the lump in my throat. He gives a distracted smile and pats Colton's shoulder. "You'll be fine in a week or so. Marsha at the front will give you a sucker for being a good elephant owner."

And then he slips out the door and into the hallway.

"He didn't say good-bye," Colton whispers. His eyebrows pinch together in consternation. "He always says bye."

I can tell that it worries him.

"Something's bothering him," I tell Colton. "I'll find out and be right back."

I open the door and head out into the hallway. It takes me a moment to locate Dr. Marchand's retreating back. I hesitate for a moment, wondering if I'm prying too much, but fuck it. I consider Dr. Marchand to be a friend of mine, and if there's something bothering him, then perhaps I can help him.

"Is everything all right?" The words leave my mouth before I can stop them, and Dr. Marchand blinks up at me. I stuff my hands into my pockets and sway on the balls of my feet, knowing that I overstepped some bounds with him. "You just seem a bit...off today."

He pauses, meeting my eyes for a brief moment before sighing and pinching the bridge of his nose. "*Non*... I mean, *oui*. I'm fine. I will be fine."

"You said no to start with," I press. Goddamn, I'm an asshole. In fact, I know I am. But, dammit, this is the man that saved my son's life, and I owe it to him.

Jacques lets out a snicker and combs a hand through his hair. "Simply problems with my visa."

"Your credit card?"

That elicits a laugh from him. "No. My visa. My ability to work legally in America."

Oh. Duh. "What happened?"

He rakes his teeth across his bottom lip. "I got my papers back today, and I was denied."

"Denied?"

He nods, and I can see the tears glisten in his eyes. "Yeah. If I don't get it sorted, I'll have to move back to France."

"Even if you don't want to?"

"Yes. I'd be an illegal alien otherwise."

Shit. "What…" I'm at a loss for words. "What about your practice here? What about your life? Haven't you been here for years?"

He chuckles sadly. "Doesn't matter if I don't have the papers to say that I'm still allowed here. Doesn't matter about anything I want."

I fight the overwhelming urge to hug him, because he seems like he needs it. "What can you do?"

"I called my lawyer and he didn't pick up." He lets out a brief laugh. "*C'est enervant.*" Even though I don't understand what he said, I have the feeling he wants to say something worse in French.

"Is there anything I can do?" I blurt. And even as I say it, I remember my vow to him two years ago, that I owe him a debt and I'd do anything for him. While the memory comes crashing through my mind, I start forming a crazy idea.

"Not unless you're an immigration officer or you have a spare green card on you," he mutters.

But I do have one of those I can give him. A spare green card.

"What if we got married?"

It's ridiculous. Insane. And it's something I can do for him. There are movies and TV shows where they do this sort of thing. I lost Jeremiah years ago. I can remarry and give Dr. Marchand a happier ending.

And it's not because he's gorgeous and you truly do want to marry him, I tell myself firmly.

He stares at me like I'm crazy. And maybe I am.

"Married?" He shakes his head. "I can't...I can't marry you. I mean..."

I glance furtively around the hospital. Luckily everyone seems to be busy with their own work and lives.

"Why not?" I ask him softly, leaning into him. I get a hint of his scent, and I have to control my baser instincts. "People scam the system all the time. You're an asset to Vale Valley and America, Dr. Marchand—*Jacques*." Saying his name causes him to give me a hard look, and I grin.

"But—"

"You saved Colton's life that day," I press. Why am I trying so hard to convince him to marry me? But charge ahead I do. "Please let me do this for you."

He considers it. I can tell he does, because he licks his lips and gets a far away look in his eyes. In the next instant, his eyes lock onto mine, clear as day.

"Thank you for your offer, *Monsieur*," he says, his accent thicker than normal now. "*Merci*, but I'll have to turn you down."

He turns on his heel and walks away, leaving me standing in the hallway.

I'm an idiot. I really am.

But I was completely serious. And I saw the desperation in his eyes, too. He knows he has options now. Just depends on if he comes to his senses.

FOUR
JACQUES

MARRY EDWIN SCHNEIDER for a green card?

It is ridiculous. Crazy. *C'est completement fou.*

How can I even be considering such a thing?

Still, though, there's some sort of appeal that keeps knocking around my head. If I cannot figure out how to solve my visa woes through the legal system and with my lawyer, it's an option.

A harebrained option. But an option, nonetheless.

"*Non,*" I mutter to myself. "I can't do that."

I think about Colton, Edwin's son, and how something like that would create an unstable environment for him. No, he needs a stepfather who will take care of him. A stepfather who will love Edwin. Who will take care of Colton like his own son?

It's not that I don't have the capacity for that. But a sham marriage is a sham marriage, and I can't believe I'm even considering this.

I leave Edwin in the hallway of the hospital and go to my office and shut the door. I'm sure I have another appointment waiting for me, but I can't keep that facade going while I have these conflicting thoughts running through my mind.

Merde.

I lean against the door and thump my head against the wood.

"I can't seriously be thinking about that," I whisper to myself.

I jump as my desk phone rings and take a moment to calm myself before I round the desk to see the caller ID. *John Wells.*

With shaking hands, I pick up the handset and bring it to my ear. "John?"

"Good morning, Dr. Marchand," my lawyer says in that voice that I had once thought was soothing, but now only irritates me. I'm blaming him for my predicament, even before I know the full extent of what's happening.

"I was denied a green card," I blurt out. "I was denied my green card, when you told me I had nothing to worry about!"

The shock on the other end is palpable. "Denied? But…"

"You said I had nothing to worry about!" I shout again, and I can't help raising my voice. "My life is ruined, John, and I'm going to have to move back to France."

"Calm down, Jacques," John says, and I close my eyes, taking as calming a breath as I can, even though my heart is racing. "We'll figure it out. Can I stop by during lunch to see what the immigration office sent you? And we'll go from there?"

I pinch the bridge of my nose, a nervous habit I picked up from years of working as a resident. "Yes. I'll clear my calendar. But…*John*…"

"Yes?"

"What if we can't fix it? What if I have to move out of the country?"

"It won't come to that, Jacques," he says. "I'll be there at noon."

He hangs up without another word, typical of a man who gets paid $400 by the hour. He doesn't waste a second. Although, it appears that he's not worth a fraction of what I've been paying him.

No, he'll fix it. He's good at what he does, and he will make this bump in the road go away.

I came to Vale Valley looking for a home and a life of my own. I'm not about to give it up without a fight.

Edwin offered to marry you for a green card.

No, it was a joke. Something offered in haste. There's nothing more to it than that.

———

AS I LEARNED LATER, hearing your lawyer say, "Fuck," is not a good thing. The couple of hours between him calling me back and him arriving has almost been too much to bear.

So to see him curse is unsettling, to say the least.

"*Excusez-moi?*" I ask, reverting back to French in my shock, unsure if I heard him correctly.

He sits across from me at my desk and flips through the letters and papers that the government sent me. John Wells is an older man in his fifties, and I've never seen him lose his cool. Yet he looks like he's about to blow a gasket as he stares at the letter.

"This can't be right," he says. "This can*not* be right."

"What happened?" I ask. "Why did they deny me?"

John ruffles his thinning hair. "Can I see your passport?"

I hand it to him, and he checks between the letters, the papers, the passport, and back again. His frown deepens more, and he manages to look more and more confused as he considers the implications of what they say.

He makes a few phone calls. I sit with growing dread in my stomach. Because as I watch him try to sort through the shambles of my life, it confirms the inevitable.

That I'm fucked.

No, not quite. A mental image of Edwin pops into my head, and I have to push it away. That doesn't count. Dammit.

"From what I can tell," John says at length, "they're saying that your waiver for working in a facility was only valid for three years."

I've been here for four. I've been working at Vale Valley General Hospital for four years, under the waiver that I don't have to go back to my home country and work for a time before I could move back to America. That waiver was meant to keep me here.

But it was only valid for three years.

I blink at him and lean forward in disbelief. "You mean to tell me that I filed my visa paperwork a year late?"

He blanches. "That's...that's what it looks like."

"But I followed your advice," I tell him. "I filed your paperwork according to your instructions." I gesture to everything on the desk. "You signed your name as my advisor! How does something like that happen?"

"I..." He gulps audibly. "I don't know."

I want to punch my hand through a wall. I'm full of bottled-up energy and I can't release it. I get up out of my chair and start pacing my office. I feel like I need to expend this energy somehow.

"Jacques," John says, looking at me. "Jacques, I'm so sorry."

"Sorry?" Sorry doesn't cut it. Sorry doesn't cover up the fact that he gave me the wrong information. Sorry doesn't make it all right. Sorry doesn't fix my life.

"What do I do, John?" I ask, throwing my hands up in the air. "I can't move back to France. Not with my life here."

All John does is look up at me with baleful eyes. "I'm sorry, Jacques."

No, no, no, no…

I'm fucked.

"*Mon Dieu.*"

———

WHAT IF WE GOT MARRIED?

That's what Edwin said. Throwing out an life preserver to save me from drowning in the ocean of despair. To save me from moving back to France.

Surely he'd been joking. Surely he didn't truly think it could work.

But…

But that may be my only option at this point.

It's not like he isn't handsome. Gorgeous. A wonderful alpha-father to his son.

I clench my teeth and suck in a deep breath through my nose. Now isn't the time to fall for the one man who gives me a hint of interest. I can't justify this by telling myself that he's wonderful and handsome.

I can't ruin his life this way.

Yet, at the same time, I mull this thought over and over in my head. I find myself fantasizing about it. I could make it up to him. He says that he is forever in my debt for saving Colton's life, but something like marrying me would...change *everything*.

I could make it up to him. I could convince myself that I love him. Heck, the attraction is already there, it wouldn't be too far to make that full leap.

Could I really marry him?

Could the American government really kick me out of the country?

The answer to the latter question is certainly yes. As for the former question, I guess it's time to see if that's a yes as well.

I take out my cell phone and scroll through my contacts to locate *Schneider*. Yes, even though I've been trying to maintain a professional/client relationship, I have his phone number in my mobile. I've even grabbed a few beers with him in the past.

There's attraction there. And I'm just about to blur the lines even further.

I hit *CALL*. The phone rings a few times before Edwin answers, and my nerves ratchet up even further.

"Schneider Classic Auto Service," he says, referring to his mechanic shop for classic cars.

"Hi, Mr. Schneider, it's Dr. Marchand." I close my eyes and curse myself. "It's *Jacques*."

"Hey, Jacques." His voice brightens, although I can tell that he's wary. "What's up?"

"Your offer." I take a deep breath and sigh. "About getting married."

"Yeah?" He sounds worried now.

I open my eyes and steel myself. "Were you serious?"

FIVE

EDWIN

"LAKELAN'S DADDY dated his stepfather a bit before they got married," Colton says with a frown as we stand outside of the Vale Valley courthouse on Valentine's Day. Lakelan is one of his best friends in school, and his dad has just gotten married to a hot alpha.

"Well, we've known Dr. Marchand for two years," I tell him. "*Jacques.*" I can now call my fiancé-to-be by his first name and no one will raise their eyebrows. "Two years is much longer than Slade knew Zach."

I hope that's enough for Colton's inquisitive mind. Because if he asks enough questions, he may blurt something to the wrong person and they start a rumor. I don't want him to lie for us, but I also don't want him to get hurt.

This whole thing moving forward is one huge gray area.

Colton's dressed in his best suit, making him look like a little man rather than a seven-year-old. And his frown certainly makes him older than he is.

"Lakelan's daddy had a baby," Colton surmises. He

peers up at me. "Is Dr. Marchand going to have a baby, too?"

"Uh." Shit.

The thought of Jacques being pregnant enters my mind, and I can't help but fantasize for a moment that he's carrying my baby and of starting a family with him.

I'm going to get into trouble if I don't rein it in. This is just for Jacques's green card. Nothing more. Not because he has feelings for me.

"I thought you didn't know where babies came from," I ask him. "How do you know about that?"

Colton giggles. "Because I'm silly."

"Yes, you are," I tell him. I sound proud, even to myself. "Will you be nice for Jacques?"

"Do I have to call him daddy?"

I hesitate, because...well, it frankly breaks my heart. Colton has always called me *daddy*, but that's because Jeremiah died when he was born. Since then, there hasn't been a need for him to consider calling any other man *daddy* or *pops* or *papa*. Or anything, really. I haven't dated anyone since Colton was born, because he's been the only man in my life.

Until now. And I'm bringing Jacques into it, a practical stranger. Never mind that I'm attracted to him, and he's gorgeous. I'm just reeling from everything.

But you're doing this as thanks for saving Colton's life.

I have to remember that and keep that distance between us.

I open my mouth to answer, but a voice interrupts me.

"No, you don't have to call me daddy."

Both Colton and I look up to see Jacques standing in front of us. Even though we're doing a small civil ceremony at the courthouse, he's dressed up in a white suit with a blue tie and his dark hair is slicked back.

He looks dapper, like he's having a big, full-blown wedding, not this fake, small one we're having.

It makes me realize that he deserves so more than what I'm giving him.

He's smiling, though, which I'll take as a good sign. He leans forward and puts his hands on his knees to bring him eye-level with Colton.

"All I ask is that you call me Jacques. Not Dr. Marchand," he says. "That would be *très étrange*."

Colton's eyes are wide. "What does that mean?"

Jacques winks. "It means *very weird* in French. I could teach you *français*, if you'd like."

Colton nodded. "Yes, please."

And just like that, Colton is fine with having a stepfather. Jacques ruffles his hair. "We'll do some practice later on today."

I shake my head, marveling. As a pediatrician, he has such a great way with kids.

Jacques meets my eyes, almost shyly, and grins. "So," he says.

"So," I say, matching his tone. Awkwardly, I reach out and hug him. I realize that's the first time I've held him like that since that day two years ago when Colton was in the hospital, and we both stay in this position. I stop myself short of double-patting him on the back. You know, the one that signals *we're just friends*.

Except we're not.

We're about to get married.

"You look great," I tell him as I step back.

He gives me a demure smile. "So do you."

God, a part of me truly hopes that. That he finds me

as handsome as I find him, because I'm finding it hard not to pounce on him and tear off that white suit of his and show him how very thankful I am that he saved Colton's life. To prove to him that I'm not just some random alpha.

I could be the alpha for him.

Right now, that scent of his is filling up my sinuses, and it seems like every breath I take is just of him. I could bottle that up and swim in it.

"Listen, *Edwin*," he says suddenly, and I stop to give him another look. He rakes his teeth on his bottom lip in the moments that pass between us, but he looks up, his eyes shining. "Thank you. You didn't have to do this."

Emotions overtake me, and I gulp back the lump in my throat. "Yes, I did," I assure him. "We're all in Vale Valley together. We help each other out. We're here for a reason. You're here for a reason. And you should stay here, too."

He licks his lips and nods. "Thank you."

"Are we ready for this?"

We both separate to see John Wells, Jacques's immigration lawyer, standing beside us. He gives us a tight grin, and I wonder what he thinks of this whole thing. Jacques said the attorney had messed up the timelines for his immigration paperwork, which is why his green card was denied.

But aren't immigration lawyers supposed to have scruples when it comes to this sort of thing?

"I'm ready," Jacques tells him, and I let out a breath. He looks back at me with a laugh. "John's here to make sure that all the papers are signed and that I can get this new application to the offices as soon as possible."

John already messed up, so I'm not sure how much I trust him not to screw this up, but here we are anyway.

I put my hand on the doorknob in front of us. "Let's do this."

He nods. "Yes."

I hold my arm out for him, and he slips his hand through the crook of my elbow. I push the door open, and we sit together in the audience, listening to the other couples that say their vows in front of the Justice of the Peace. Appropriately, it's Valentine's Day, which means that there are plenty of couples and thruples saying their vows. Vale Valley may be a small town, but romance is definitely in the air.

I just wish it were that case between Jacques and me.

Then it's our turn. We make our way to the front of the room, with Colton in tow. We exchange our vows. Colton, as my best man and ring bearer, hands me the simple wedding bands I purchased at the local jeweler's. I slip the ring on Jacques's hand, and he does the same for me. We sign the papers—the important ones that Jacques will use for immigration applications.

And then comes the awkward part. I knew it was coming, I just haven't prepared myself for it or figured out what I'll do during it.

But the Justice of the Peace grins at us and says, "I now you pronounce you husband and husband. You may now kiss."

Both Jacques and I stare at each other for a moment. Apparently, he hasn't considered what to do at this point either. For a strange, weird moment, I wonder if weddings go the same way in France as they do in America. Maybe they don't end with kissing.

Then again, Jacques has lived here for four years, I'm sure he's familiar with how weddings end here.

I lick my lips. I feel my heart pound.

Make it look natural. Make it look like he is the love of your life.

I can do that.

I just go for it. I lean forward and catch his lips with mine. They're softer than I thought they'd be, supple and full. At first, he doesn't open his mouth to me, and I wonder if this is going to be one of those chaste kisses that you see awkward couples do. The ones who don't truly love each other.

Then his arms come around my back and hold me to him. His lips part, and I slip my tongue inside, tasting him. And oh, god, does he taste wonderful. There's a sound and I think it's one of us moaning. If not both of us.

His lips sear against mine, and when I finally step back to draw breath, he looks just as dazed as I feel.

What was that?

The Justice of the Peace's eyes are wide open, her mouth in a little *O*. "Wow," she says. "You two must really love each other."

And my cheeks blush, and they don't stop until we leave the courthouse.

SIX

JACQUES

OH, *merde!*

That was the hottest kiss of my life. Between my fake husband and me, whom I never kissed before our wedding. And as he takes my hand and leads me away from the Justice of the Peace, toward a fake future together, I wonder if it truly has to be that.

A fake future.

Can't it be more real? Is there anything that says I can't follow through with my feelings?

I've always found Edwin to be a good-looking man. A man who loves his son more than life itself. A part of me is shocked that he wants to repay a supposed debt for saving Colton's life.

Another part of me wishes it were more than that.

Edwin doesn't meet my eyes as we head out to the steps of the courthouse. As if he's embarrassed. Or distracted. Or maybe the kiss grossed him out.

The thought of him disliking the kiss makes my heart twist horribly in my chest. Like it wants to break. Which is ridiculous, as I'm not supposed to have feelings for him.

I'm not supposed to care about him beyond our arrangement.

"Daddy?" Colton asks in alarm. "What's wrong?"

He rubs at his lips. Those lips that I kissed. "Nuh-nothing, Colton. I'm just thinking."

Thinking about what? I want to ask him.

"You kissed Jacques," Colton says with a giggle. "Like kissy face and everything."

Kissy face indeed. I look over to Edwin, who keeps rubbing at his lips, as if he's lost in thought.

"Should we get a picture?" John asks as he takes out his phone. "The immigration office likes it when you have pictures together. And a shared bank account," he adds as an afterthought, and Edwin flinches at that.

He's a mechanic, and I'm a pediatrician. Not that a mechanic's salary is anything to sniff at and I really don't care about money, but I don't want him feeling awkward at seeing my paychecks.

We haven't discussed that part, though. Really, this whole thing has been such a whirlwind, we haven't discussed much other than Colton and Edwin moving into my house in a couple of days.

To the outside eye, we're madly in love and eloping, caught up in the kind of romance that you read in books. To us, we're just floundering, trying to figure out how to pretend to be married.

We're either doing too good of a job or not a good enough one. I wish we could find the middle ground.

"We can do the picture," I tell John, trying to assuage Edwin's embarrassment, "but I'm not doing the shared bank account. A lot of couples keep that separate nowadays."

John considers this and then shrugs. "You sure?" He jogs a few steps ahead of us and kneels to snap a picture.

"I don't want him seeing how much I'm paying you," I mutter, giving him a blithe smile. "Especially since you messed up my paperwork in the first place."

Which is why he's doing this part for free and being so nice to me. Because he owes me big time. *Zut*, he probably should be the one marrying me for the green card to make up for his mistakes, but I'm in this arrangement with Edwin, which...I'm finding that I'm liking.

He's handsome. Has a nice, tight *derrière*. And he loves his son.

What omega wouldn't love that?

"Say *frommage*," John says with a laugh.

"What?" Colton asks, looking up at us.

"He means *cheese*," Edwin says with a laugh. He hugs him to him and puts his arms around my shoulders. "Smile for the camera."

I do, feeling oddly turned on at the proximity of the alpha's body close to mine. I force a smile, not because it's hard to pretend that I have feelings for Edwin, but because my cock stiffens at his touch on my shoulders.

Dammit, I'm getting too far into this.

John snaps a few photos in landscape and portrait format and comes up the stairs to show me the pictures. "Y'all look like a loving family."

I take the phone from him and blink rapidly a few times. Because he's right. Edwin, Colton, and I look like the perfect family. All that's missing is a white picket fence.

"What do you think?" I ask, holding the phone down for Colton to see. The boy takes it from me, and his eyes widen, along with a huge grin.

"You look like two daddies," he says. He looks up at me

as he hands the phone back. "You look like you're my new daddy."

Which is exactly what I hope the immigration officers will see, but I suddenly feel conflicted for Colton. What does this tell him about love and happiness?

Don't be an asshole to him. Show him that you're still a good man.

And once I meet all the qualifications for my green card, I can extricate myself from this family, hopefully leaving as little scarring as possible on Colton. Colton, who has a step-father because of an arrangement with his alpha-father.

But you don't want to leave, do you? Deep down, you want this to work out.

And it's that thought that scares me.

I meet Edwin's eyes and he gives me an encouraging me. "We did it," he says breathlessly. "We got married."

Then, catching both of us off guard, he leans forward and presses those petal-soft lips against my forehead. I close my eyes and sigh into him, relishing it. Maybe it's for show or maybe he's caught up in the moment, but I can't help but feel safe in his arms.

"We have a Valentine's dinner and reception," he reminds me as he steps back. "All our friends will be there."

Friends who believe that we're truly in love and eloping. John is the only one who knows this is a sham. Here's to client confidentiality, and I hope that stays true.

But the next test will be proving to our friends that we love each other. At least enough to make a rash decision.

I entwine my fingers in Edwin's hands and give it a quick squeeze. "Let's do it, *mon mari.*"

He frowns in confusion. "What does that mean?"

"It means, *my husband.*"

———

"AND TO THINK, this entire time that Colton was seeing you, you were dating his father!" Marsha says in too loud of a voice with a chuckle. I think she's had a little bit too much to drink at our reception. "How long has this been in the works?"

"Oh, well, you know," I say with a nonchalant shrug. I meet Edwin's eyes across the room of the restaurant as he talks with some other friends of we share in common. "It's been going on for about two years now."

Which, oddly, is the truth. Because that's when Edwin promised his debt to me.

"Two years," Marsha sighs. "You have been so good about hiding it."

"Well, you know people frown on doctors dating their patients' fathers." I let out a chuckle. "I didn't want people talking."

"Oh, people are talking, but not because of that," she interjects. "We're just all sad that not one, but *two* eligible bachelors are out of the running now."

I laugh. "Marsha, no offense, but you were never our type." She's a nice woman and everything, but I've always been interested in alphas, and I'm sure Edwin is the same in regards to omegas.

She only laughs and shakes her head. "Well, if you or Edwin have brothers who *are* interested in women, send them my way."

"And my way, too!" another nurse from my work shouts, and the entire restaurant erupts into laughter.

Edwin and I meet each other's eyes again, and I find that everyone is pushing us closer and closer together.

"Kiss!" someone shouts, and I can't tell if they're Edwin's friend or my own.

But that one command creates a chant, and suddenly everyone is telling us to *kiss, kiss, kiss!*

Edwin takes my hand and squeezes it. He raises his eyebrow in invitation.

Don't mind if I do.

I reach up and cup his face to mine, gently brushing my lips against his. It's our second kiss, shared in front of our friends and family. And it feels just as earth-shattering as the first one.

He kisses me fervently. The flare of passion that ignites between us surprises me and I cling to him out of fear that I'll catch fire as well. The heat that's there is intense, and I'm in his arms, feeling him up against me.

Then I feel the hard outline of his cock pressed against my thigh. He's just as turned on by this as I am.

He steps back, that same heat sweltering in his eyes as he searches my face.

And for a moment, a thought shocks me.

I think I'm falling in love with my husband.

SEVEN

EDWIN

I HATE MOVING.

Hate it with a passion, but Jacques promised me that I wouldn't have to pay rent to live in his house, which is one of the benefits of marrying him. Not that I had agreed to marry him for the free rent—I wouldn't have changed a thing.

Still though, the immigration office likes to see that we're cohabiting together, and Jacques's house is much larger than the apartment I rent over my garage, so moving in together we are, moving the day after Valentine's.

I just have to remind myself that there are more perks that I'm getting out of this instead of sore muscles and a bad back.

Jacques has a dog, an adorable pug named Carlin that Colton immediately takes a shining to. From the moment we show up, Colton immediately drops his box and catches the barking little dog in his hands.

"It's like Christmas!" he giggles, as the scrunch-faced canine leaves slobbery kisses all over him. Jacques had warned me about his ill-mannered dog, but I can't help but chuckle as the little dog attacks my son in the most endearing way.

"He probably needs to go outside," Jacques says, giving me a knowing wink. "And he loves it if you throw a ball, too."

"Really?" Colton's face lights up for a moment, before Carlin jumps up and licks him all over the place.

"*Oui*," Jacques says with a nod.

"Can I, Daddy?" Colton asks. And I know his hesitation is because we're in a new house, so his politeness comes from that, but still...

"Hey," I say, setting down a box. "It's your house. And he's your dog now, too."

Colton's shriek of happiness is ear-splitting, and I'm almost relieved when he sprints out the door, the pug in tow behind him.

"Shut the door behind you!" I call to him, and there's an answering slam as he does just that. I give Jacques an apologetic smile. "Sorry about that, he's always wanted a dog."

"Trust me," Jacques says, "Carlin loves the attention. This old omega doesn't play with him as much as he should." He sets down a box and straightens with a wince. "One of the perks of being on my insurance, by the way," he adds, "is massages are included. Which will be good after this move."

I smirk. "You're not going to give me one?"

Shit, that left my mouth before I considered the implications of it, and I can practically hear Jacques gulp uncomfortably.

"Sorry," I say awkwardly. "Bad joke."

"*Non,*" he says, shaking his head. "Don't worry about it."

But I do worry about it. Especially since we are going to be sharing a roof with each other. I press my lips together, but I don't know what to say, other than extend this awkwardness.

"I'll go get more boxes," I say, heading out to the moving truck. Where, hopefully, Jacques can't see me sweating profusely.

———

I DIDN'T THINK Colton and I had much stuff after selling most of our furniture, but four hours later, Jacques and I finally bring in all the boxes from the moving truck. I'm apparently out of shape, because my entire body aches from all the heavy lifting.

Luckily, Colton has been outside the entire time, playing with an over-enthusiastic Carlin. I have the feeling that my son and the dog are going to sleep well tonight.

Hell, I have the feeling that I'm going to fall face first into bed and not get up for a week. That sounds absolutely divine.

"Hey," Jacques says, "go shower. Doctor's orders." He smiles at me, and my heart does a flip flop. Despite our awkward moments as a married couple, we do seem to get along really well, and he seems to be in tune with help when I need it.

"A shower sounds great," I mutter, rubbing the back of my neck.

"Use the shower in the master bedroom," Jacques prompts. "It has a massage function."

"That would be amazing," I murmur, even as I still at him saying *the master bedroom*. He and I are going to sleep in separate rooms, me and Colton in the master bedroom while he stays in the guestroom. He says it makes more sense, since there will be two people who need the larger master bedroom.

But, this is Jacques's house. He deserves more than that.

"Go on," he says, giving me a gentle push in the direction of the master bedroom. My bedroom-to-be.

The house feels huge, even with Colton's and my stuff scattered all over the place. For three people and a dog, it's too big. I can't even imagine how empty it must have felt with just Jacques and Carlin here, alone.

Bringing Colton here, it feels like we're giving the place some character.

I find the nice shower with the glass door and strip off my sweaty, stinky clothes. It takes a little bit of finagling to get the shower to turn on, but once I do, I can tell that the intense water pressure and the different jets will be just what I need to feel better.

I open the glass door and step into the steamy embrace of the shower and sigh contentedly. "Oh, yes," I mutter to myself. "That feels so good."

And indeed, it does feel so good. I lean forward into the spray of the water, feeling the water pummel my aching muscles into submission. I brace one hand against the wall and let the water cascade down my face.

So wonderful. In fact, the only way it could be better is if I were sharing it with someone.

Someone like your husband, perhaps, a voice in the back of my mind tells me, a dangerous voice that makes me open my eyes and my cock stiffen. Because I would want Jacques to join me in here, to fulfill that massage that I had teased about earlier.

I'm such an asshole.

But I can't chide myself for too long. My cock grows ever more hard and painful, and I reach down and give it a long, steady stroke.

Yes, that feels good.

And I do it again.

And again.

And before I know it, I'm building up a rhythm, stroking myself, bringing me ever closer to the edge. My imagination wanders as well, because I figure that I'm in the privacy of my bathroom. I'm in the house where I live. I've been holding back these thoughts for a while now, and maybe getting it out of my system will be a good thing.

I imagine Jacques joining me in the hot steamy shower. And in my fantasy, he's naked as well, his hard, uncircumcised cock at the ready.

"*Bonjour, mon mari,*" he purrs to me. "*Parlez-vous français?*"

"*Oui,*" I tell him, and I pretend that my hand is his as he kneels in front of me and takes me in his mouth. "*Oui,*" I breathe, and the fantasy feels almost as good as what I think the real thing could be.

"Does my alpha like that?" he asks.

"*Oui,*" I say again.

He starts sucking me harder now, and I move quickly to mimic the movement in mind. Sucking and cupping my balls. I start saying the only words that I know in French that seem appropriate.

"*Oui…Merci…Oui…Merci…Oui…Oui…*"

Goddammit, I need to learn more French for my fantasies if I'm going to keep doing this. But I hold onto that image of Jacques's handsome face sucking me off, and I start going faster. Finally, I come, spurting my seed all over the tile of the shower.

"*Oui, Jacques!*"

I stand there for a moment, heaving great breaths, trying to get my pulse under control. I can't believe I just did that. And I called out Jacques's name. Hopefully, he didn't hear me. Hopefully…

"Edwin!"

Fuck.

"Um, I'm just in here," I say, my voice somewhat strangled. I grab the towel and try to wrap it out around my waist, but my knot is still there, evidence of what I just did. The terry cloth does little to hide that fact, too, and the glass door gives me nowhere to hide.

"You said my name—" he says as he enters the bathroom, and he stops. His eyes go to my face, and then to my engorged knot. "*Mon Dieu,*" he says in shock.

I turn around, showing him my back. "Sorry about that," I mutter embarrassedly.

I don't hear movement from him, meaning that he's still standing there, gaping at me. Dammit, I wish the ground would open up and swallow me. And even though it's steamy in here, I'm sure he can see the spurts of white dripping down the wall.

"Sorry to bother you," he says quickly, and then I hear the door shut behind him.

Dammit, dammit, dammit.

I pass a hand over my face, still heaving from my extracurricular activities.

Well, that's fucking awkward.

EIGHT

JACQUES

I CAUGHT Edwin masturbating in the shower. And as if that's not enough, he called my name. Like I was a part of his fantasy.

And I don't have the balls to ask him or to follow through with the fantasy. Even though it's something I want—because, yes, I've decided that I want him. I want him more than I've wanted anything in my life.

Including a green card. Including my practice.

The reason why I don't do anything more is because I don't want to ruin what Edwin and I do have. With this arrangement, we're meant to be kept separate. Apart from everything.

And there's a line I'm not sure is healthy to cross at this point. I don't know if Edwin just did that out of curiosity. To maybe imagine what sex would be like with me.

And maybe he decided he didn't like it, because he gave me no further indication to continue.

The rest of the night is awkward. Colton and Carlin come in from outside, exhausted from a day spent outdoors. The boy doesn't even have dinner before he falls asleep in the master bedroom. Edwin and I spend the rest of the time actively trying to avoid each other.

"Well," I say awkwardly, getting to my feet. "Good night."

Edwin bites his lip, and I avert my eyes. *He's trying to figure out how to smooth over the awkwardness. Not say anything else.*

"Jacques," he says, and my heart leaps to my throat.

I turn back to him, hopeful. "*Oui?*"

Apparently, saying *yes* in my native language is the wrong thing to do, because his cheeks turn bright red and his eyes shutter close.

"Have a good night," he says awkwardly. "Thank you for letting us stay here."

I nod. "You're welcome. Thank you for stepping in. And being my husband for immigration."

He smiles somberly. "It's what's right," he says. "You're an asset to Vale Valley. If we lost you, every child in the town would be fucked."

Is that the only reason why he wants me here? Not for other reasons?

I smile. "We both have things that we're working toward," I tell him softly. And I leave him in the living room and head back to the guest room that I now call my own.

Underneath the covers, I find that my cock is throbbing, wanting release.

I close my ears and take all of two seconds to debate what to do. I wrap my hand around my shaft and start jacking myself off. Because if my husband can use a fantasy of me to get off, then I can do the same.

I sleep very well that night, because Edwin is in my every thought. And I wrap his image around me like a warm blanket.

"OH! PERFECT TIMING, DR. MARCHAND!" Marsha says as I head toward my office in the morning. She has the phone receiver in the crook of her shoulder and swivels in her chair to follow me. She puts her hand over the mouthpiece. "You have an Officer Wagner on the phone for you."

I frown. "Officer Wagner?"

The name isn't familiar. Usually, any time I have to deal with law enforcement, it has to do with a patient that I'm treating. Those are the toughest cases, cases that I shudder to think about.

"She says it's in regards to your immigration application," Marsha says off-handedly. She doesn't seem worried. And why would she be? After all, in her eyes, I'm married to the love of my life and I shouldn't dread talking with them.

In her eyes, anyway.

Meanwhile, for me, it's happening much, much faster than I had pictured.

Merde.

"I'll take that in my office," I tell her, giving her a tight-lipped smile. "Tell her I'll be right on the phone."

"Dr. Marchand will be right with you," she says into the phone. She gives a smart nod and hits the button to transfer it to my office.

I have about thirty seconds to rehearse and figure out what I'm going to say to an immigration officer. Thirty seconds to sound like everything is fine.

But nothing coming to mind, because I'm fucked.

I close my office door behind me and take a deep

breath. The phone on my desk is already ringing. I count to three before I pick it up.

"This is Dr. Marchand," I say, hoping I sound as matter-of-factly as I'm trying to be. "How can I help you?"

"Hello, Dr. Marchand, this is Officer Wagner with the U.S. Citizenship and Immigration Services," the woman says on the other end. She sounds like a no-nonsense kind of woman, which I suppose comes with the territory. "How are you doing today?"

"Fine, thanks," I say. "How can I help you, officer?"

"I'm just reviewing your newly-submitted application for a green card, Dr. Marchand," she says at length, almost like she's reading it as she looks at me. "It appears that you submitted an application for a spousal visa right after you got married two days ago."

"I'm surprised your office is already looking at the paperwork," I tell her honestly. "I sent it out that day."

"Well, especially in cases where we have denied green cards in the past for one reason, we investigate subsequent applications for fraud." I can almost hear her devious smile on the other end. "Now, why would you apply for a green card after the HB-1 waiver, when you could have done a fiancé visa in the first place?"

I've rehearsed this. John and I have gone over this answer a dozen times.

"That was a mistake on my lawyer's part," I say. "I miscommunicated with him that I wanted to apply under a fiancé visa, and he went and applied under another scheme."

"Rare that things like that happen," she says, sounding unconvinced.

"Well, I think he's out of practice," I say. "He mostly deals in divorces."

She lets out a sharp laugh. "And so you sought to remedy that with this application? Did you marry Mr. Edwin Schneider because of the application denial or was that already in place?"

Another question I've been rehearsing for. "It was already in place. We'd wanted to have a Valentine's wedding." Again, it's a logical answer.

"Strange that you would plan so much only for it to take place at the courthouse. I'm looking at a copy of your marriage certificate right now. It was a pretty small event, wasn't it? Not quite the big blowout of a wedding."

I let out a breath. "Well, Edwin has been married once before. And I didn't want something big—people always blow their weddings out of proportion. With Edwin having a son from his first marriage, we wanted to be smart about it and make sure that we didn't go overboard."

"I agree." I blink in surprise at her admission. "My own wedding was small, too. It's the way to go."

"It is, indeed," I say. I run a hand through my hair. "Is this the only reason why you're calling me, Officer Wagner?"

"I'm just following up with everything," she says, sounding like she's bored. "Making sure that yours is a legitimate marriage."

"It is," I tell her through clenched teeth. I stop short of telling her that both Edwin and I consummated our marriage. Granted, it was at different times. And in fantasies. But that has to account for something, right?

"And do you live with Mr. Schneider?" she asks.

"He just moved in yesterday," I say. "With his son Colton. They're already settled in."

"Sounds like life is moving beautifully." There's a long pause. "Dr. Marchand, as a courtesy, I wanted to let you know that I'll be investigating your case to make sure that you are in a true relationship with Edwin."

I gulp. "I understand."

"That includes reaching out to your friends and family," Officer Wagner continues. "And possibly an interview between you and Mr. Schneider."

Merde. "It makes sense. You don't want there to be immigration fraud."

"Correct." She sounds like she's smiling again. "I'll be in touch, Dr. Marchand."

And she hangs up. I look at the phone for a long moment before slamming it into the cradle. I default to English for the harshest curse words, and I mutter them under my breath as I rub at my eyes.

"*Fuck, fuck, fuck, fuck!*"

I TELL Marsha that I'm not feeling very well and that I can't take my appointments for the rest of the day. It's a weak lie, like everything in my life, but I can't pretend like everything is all right.

So I leave the hospital and go to the only person I can talk to about this.

I'm a bundle of nerves by the time I make it to Edwin's classic autobody shop across town via the bus. I keep replaying my conversation with Officer Wagner over and over in my head. What I said. What she said. And how everything could be interpreted.

She knows. And she's going to arrest me and deport me.

"*Non,*" I tell myself, shaking my head. "*Non.*"

When I walk up to the shop, the garage door is open, and there's an old Firebird parked on the right side, the hood propped open. Edwin is bent over to work on the insides of the vehicles, and for a moment, I'm struck by how similar our careers are, even though they look to be as different as night and day.

We both have to diagnose and treat problems that ail our patients. Mine just happen to be children and his are old automobiles.

But we're more similar than I ever could have guessed.

Edwin looks up as I approach him, and he frowns at me. "Jacques?" he asks. He wipes his greasy hands on a rag. Big hands. Hands that could comfort me. "Jacques, what's wrong?"

What's wrong?

Zut, I don't even know that. I just feel exposed and in danger from my phone call with Officer Wagner. I feel as though I've created a problem for all of us, and I can't fix it.

The worst part? I do have feelings for Edwin. Even though this is a sham marriage, I care for him. The kisses we've shared have been ground-breaking. I love how he cares for Colton. I love how he's true and stands by his word.

I'm starting to love *him*.

There's only one thing I can do right now to calm the raging storm inside my head.

I walk right up to him and plant a huge kiss on his lips.

And I'm lost to him.

NINE

EDWIN

JACQUES IS KISSING ME.

Here.

In front of my shop.

There's no one to see him do that. No one to have to pretend in front of. We don't have to pretend like we're the happily married couple we try to be.

No. It's just him and me in the morning. He's kissing me like the world is about to end for him. And I know that I want to do everything in my power to make him feel safe.

We break for air, and we're both panting. I cup his cheeks, looking him deep in the eyes. "Jacques," I breathe, "Jacques, what's wrong?"

"I don't want this to be a sham marriage," he tells me. His eyes sparkle with unshed tears. "I don't want to pretend anymore."

For a moment, I think he's trying to get out of being married to me. Which is ridiculous, considering that he's visiting me during work hours to kiss me like he's never kissed anyone before. Then I wonder what happened to make him act this way.

"Don't want to pretend, how?" I ask, trying to make sure that I'm interpreting everything correctly. Because, for all I know, this has nothing to do with where I think it's going.

Jacques meets my eyes and holds me there for a long moment. "I'm...attracted to you, Edwin," he says softly. "You say that you married me for a debt, so that I can get my green card. You say that's all we are. But..." His voice trails off, leaving me wondering.

"But what?"

He meets my eyes again. "But that kiss we shared at the wedding. The dinner. Last night at my house..."

My cheeks flush with embarrassment. So he *did* see everything I did in the shower.

But he keeps going, to my wonder. "You're a wonderful alpha, Edwin, someone who deserves to be treated like a king. You *and* Colton. You deserve to be happy, not have me drag you down. Not with immigration thinking it's a lie. I could never forgive myself if you were caught up in my problems."

"So you want out of the marriage?" I ask, feeling that icy pit in my stomach. It's only been three days since we exchanged vows, and he's already having regrets. That has to be some sort of record, right? One I never wanted to break. "Jacques..."

"*Non,*" he says quickly and shakes his head. "No, it's not that. It's..." He closes his eyes and lets out a breath. "I care about you, Edwin. More than I should. And if you don't feel that way, then..."

He cares for me. I stare at him, shocked, wondering if I heard his words correctly. Because he cares about me, and he's here because he wants to hear it from me, too.

"Do you...love me, Jacques?" I ask softly.

Our eyes meet again as his bottom lip trembles. "I think I could," he says, before letting out a short laugh and shaking his head. "I really, truly think I could, and I don't want our fake marriage to make everything else fake. I don't want you thinking I'm fake."

"Oh, Jacques," I whisper. And before I can stop myself, I rush forward and kiss him again. He clings to me, trembling with the weight of his confession. I break the kiss, just momentarily, so I can assure him that his feelings are returned. I say the words that I just learned this morning on my way in to work, because I didn't want the extent of my French to be *oui* and *merci*.

"Omega," I tell him, emotion making my voice rough, "*je t'aime.*"

He stares at me in wonder for a long moment, before a wide grin pulls at his lips. "*Je t'aime,*" he whispers back.

I kiss him again, and this time, we're both on equal footing. His mouth is open and his tongue explores my space as I do the same to him. This kiss is the most primitive, most wanton yet.

And, suddenly, I don't want it to stop. Not here.

I pull him to me, within the overhang of the autoshop and reach for the button to close the electric garage door. Somehow, even with him nibbling at my bottom lip, I'm able to find it and hit the button. The door jolts and starts to slide down, enclosing Jacques and me in the space, along with the Firebird.

"I want you, omega," I growl to him as I start to undo his tie and the buttons of his dress shirt. Dammit, doctors always have to have so many different articles of clothing on. Meanwhile, I'm here in a t-shirt and jeans. "I want you bent over the hood of the Firebird as I pound you in the ass."

"*Oui*," he tells me, and I can't help smiling, because that's exactly how my fantasy went with him last night. "Will we get caught?"

I shake my head, although the possibility of it sends a thrill through me. I want to chide him for worrying and for stopping to ask that. "No, we can't get caught. I'm working alone today."

And thank fuck for that.

I manage to peel of his shirt, and I see the bare expanse of his chest. As a doctor, he's taken great care of his body over the years, and I trail my fingers down the curves his muscles create. Damn, he's beautiful. He has no idea, either. And that innocence just turns me on.

I bite his nipple, hard, and he lets out gasp. "That's right, omega mine," I mutter to him. "Your pleasure is mine. Your body is mine. If you'll let me."

"*Oui*," he says, his voice a cross between a longing sigh and something else. "*Oui*, I'm yours."

I strip off my shirt and undo the buckle and fly of my jeans. He caught a glimpse of my cock last night, but this is the first time he's seen it up close and ready especially for him. His eyebrows raise in appreciation before he smiles at me.

"You're big," he tells me.

"For you," I tell him. "I'm hard for you." I stroke the tip of my cock, feeling the precum bead there. "This is all for you, omega mine."

He takes the hint and falls to his knees. He first licks the offering I'm giving him, like I'm the most delicious ice cream cone he's ever tasted. In response, my body produces more precum, and he grins wickedly. Just like in my fantasy last night, he takes me fully in his mouth, and I grasp at the car to keep my balance.

"Oh, *fuck*," I mutter as his head bobs up and down my length.

My fantasy may have been of him doing this last night, but fantasy never amounts to the real thing. This is something else entirely. Wonderful, beautiful, and it's a symphony of our bodies working together.

He sucks me until I nearly come. But no, this is our first time together. I'm not going to finish in his mouth. Not this way. Not without me appreciating his body too.

"Jacques," I say. I put a hand to his head, meaning to stop him. "Jacques. I want you bent over the car. I want to finish inside you and to fill you up with my cum."

He stops blowing me, and looks up at me with my cock still in his mouth. I feel the muscles of his mouth shift around me as he smiles. Finally he breaks contact with me, and I nearly sob at the feeling of losing him like this.

But no, I'm not losing him. I'm taking him in the way he deserves.

"Your trousers," I tell him. "Off. Now."

He obliges me, slipping off those black slacks quick, and exposing his tight ass and well-muscled thighs. An ass and thighs I want to bite.

To my delight, I find that my fantasy from last night is right once again. He's uncircumcised, and his cock is something to behold.

I'm the luckiest alpha on earth.

"Over the car," I say roughly as I put the hood down. "Bend over the car, and spread your feet shoulder-width apart."

He does so without another word. Just to make sure he's ready for me, I slip a finger inside his entrance. He's wet for me, to my continued joy. "Oh, you're so slick, omega. Do I make you slick?"

"*Oui*," he says again. He mutters something else in French, but I barely hear it as I slip another finger inside him.

"How about that?"

"*Oui*," he whines again.

I reach around him and grab his hard cock in my free hand. His velvety skin is already so taut, so hard. I stroke him once and he lets out a cry.

"And that, omega mine?"

"*Oui*." I slip another finger inside him, and before I can ask if he likes that, he says, "*Oui*," again.

Fuck, I don't think I can last much longer.

"I'm going to fuck you in the ass, omega mine," I tell him. "And I want you to describe what I'm doing to you in French. I want you to tell me how that makes you feel. How much you like it. And how much you want it." I slip in a fourth finger and he moans. "Can you do that for me, omega mine?"

"*Oui*," he says, and his legs are trembling.

In one swift movement, I take out my fingers, position my cock at his opening, and slam myself home. He arches his head back and lets out a strangled cry. I slam into him again.

"In French," I remind him. "Tell me what I'm doing to you in French."

He nods once, before he breaks out into French, his words stringing together in a rhythm that I match. I gain a new appreciation for the language, how its delicate syllables lace together to create something so romantic and so erotic. I use it as my way to drive him over the edge.

He lets out a cry, and I see the he spurts cum on the wheel of the Firebird. He came for me. I did this to him.

And that realization makes me orgasm as well. I cry

out his name and slam into his hips one last time as I empty myself into him. For he is a good omega, and I want to take care of him. To make sure that he knows he's appreciated.

I keep my knot inside him, holding him to me, although we both seem a bit woozy on our feet. He licks his lips as he looks at me, his expression full of that same heat.

"*Je t'aime,*" he whispers to me.

I kiss him in answer. "*Je t'aime,*" I say back to him.

Forever and ever.

TEN

JACQUES

I'M in love with my husband.

Such a strange feeling to admit it to myself and to him, especially after we're already married, but it's true.

It's so true.

There's a certain relief in knowing that everything has fallen into place, that despite the original arrangement, despite the distance that it could have created, we have crossed that ocean. I know that he cares for me as much as I care for him. I'm certain of it.

Especially since we can't keep our hands off each other.

After our initial session of lovemaking in his garage, he had his way with me in the waiting room of his shop. And then on every surface of my house. Of *our* house, as I've come to think of it.

After that initial night spent in separate rooms, I move back into the master bedroom, where we sleep with Colton and Carlin snuggled up between us. It's an odd mixture of a family, one that I didn't see coming, but there it is.

Officer Wagner, the immigration officer, can do her

investigations and her interviews. I have nothing to fear since Edwin's and my relationship is true and solid.

We just happened to be married before we fell in love.

I'm thinking about that as I watch the sun rise from our bed, feeling wonderfully content. Oh, sure, I have Colton's knee in my side—the boy can't sleep without elbowing both of us in the face at least once—and Carlin keeps twitching at odd moments.

But this is a better reality than I could have ever imagined it.

I sigh contentedly.

"What are you thinking about?"

I turn my head at Edwin's voice to find him lazily smiling at me from the other side of our king-sized bed. He's shirtless, and I can see the planes of his chest and his stomach outlined beneath the sheet.

"I'm thinking about how life can be funny," I tell him.

He props himself up on his elbow and raises a quizzical eyebrow. "Funny how?"

I let out a chuckle. "Funny in that you can have a crazy idea that works out wonderfully."

He snickers softly and ruffles Colton's hair. "So you're afterglowing."

"Afterglowing with life," I correct him. I slowly trace the area around his exposed nipple, and he hisses a sharp intake of breath. "Also I was thinking about how Colton's knee in my ribs is going to give me another bruise."

He grimaces. "Sorry about that. It's just that with Jeremiah gone, I don't want him to feel alone. Ever."

I cup a hand to his cheek. "And I wasn't saying that Colton's knee in my ribs is a bad thing," I tell him. "It's my new reality. One that I didn't see coming, but I love it nonetheless."

He turns his face and kisses the palm of my hand. "How did I end up with such a wonderful omega like you?"

I grin at him. "Well, you were highly insistent about owing a debt to me."

"You stopped a bus for Colton and saved his life. What father wouldn't want to make it up to his son's savor?"

"That's because you're a wonderful man," I whisper to him, and I mean it.

As if he knew we were talking about him, Colton groans and shifts in his sleep, turning toward his alpha-father and curling up against his side. Carlin stretches in his sleep as well, and snores loudly. Both Edwin and I chuckle softly.

Silly pug.

I sigh contentedly and rub at the sore spot in my side from Colton's knee.

I was telling the truth about it all. That everything is just how I want it to be.

Then I taste the bile in my throat. Rising unexpectedly and quickly.

Merde.

"What is it?" Edwin asks in alarm as I get up from the bed and run to the bathroom. I barely make it to the toilet before I vomit up everything in my stomach from the night before. I groan and sink to my knees as I hug the commode.

"Jacques?" Edwin stands in the doorway, and I twist my head to peer up at him. "Are you okay, omega mine?"

I wipe my mouth with the back of my hand. "*Oui.*" I let a short laugh, which is a mistake, because my stomach threatens to rebel again. "I think I have food poisoning from last night."

Edwin stares at me for a long moment before smirking. I frown at him.

"What?"

"Oh, omega mine," he says as he comes over to me. "You're not sick. At least not in the way you're thinking."

My frown deepens. "*Comment cela?*" I ask him, and he raises an eyebrow at my French. I shake my head and regret that as well. "What do you mean?" I amend.

He kneels next to me and puts an arm around my shoulders. "You haven't been through this before. But I have."

I wait for him to stop speaking in riddles.

"You're pregnant, Jacques."

His words echo in the bathroom, and I both understand them and don't at the same time. I stare him for a long moment, processing what he just told me.

Pregnant.

"What?" I ask. "How?"

He rubs my back soothingly. "Oh, my love, you may be a doctor, but here I am, the one who's diagnosing you." He nibbles my ear, even though I'm certain that I smell like sick still. "Think about it. We've been married for six weeks now. You've been moody lately."

"I have not been moody!" I say.

He presses a kiss to my temple. "And you've been getting 'food poisoning' a lot lately. Think about it. Really think about it, my love."

I do. I think back to that first time six weeks ago in Edwin's garage and how we've been making love like there's no tomorrow. We haven't used protection that entire time. Of course the odds of me being pregnant would be high.

I'm a doctor who apparently doesn't know how babies are made.

My eyes fill with tears. "Oh, Edwin."

He kisses my forehead. "I've suspected it for a few days now," he tells me gently. "I thought you knew. I thought you were saving the news for a special time."

I snicker softly, even as the tears fall down my cheeks. "No," I admit. "I had no idea. I just…"

He gives me a tense, almost frightened look. "I…I hope you're okay with it," he tells me softly. "That you're okay with carrying my child."

I put a hand to his cheek. "Of course I am!" I tell him. "*Mon mari*, of course I am. I am just scared. And shocked. But mostly scared."

He touches his forehead to mine, and I close my eyes, feeling the close proximity of his body to mine. How close he is. How much I love him.

"That's natural," he tells me. "And I'll be here for you. During your pregnancy and beyond. I'll be here for you and our baby." With one hand, he puts a flat palm on my stomach. It shows no sign of the child that I'm carrying, but soon.

Soon…

"I love you so much," I tell him.

He brushes at my cheeks with his thumb. And then he picks me up and carries me to the shower, where he shows me just how appreciative he is that I'm carrying his child. He makes me come again and again, worshipping my body in a way that only Edwin can.

And I can't remember a single moment where I've ever been more happy.

ELEVEN

EDWIN

"MON PETIT CHOU," Jacques murmurs in wonder, touching the ultrasound of our nineteen-week old baby. We're driving back from the doctor's office, where we had our check-up of our baby. Before Colton, I'd always thought of ultrasounds as being indecipherable scratches on a computer screen, but there's something different about seeing your own baby and hearing its heartbeat. I imagine that it's the same for Jacques, as this is his first baby.

There's a difference in seeing the most precious thing in the world to you on the screen for the first time. He's acted like he's been enamored with the baby this entire time.

And I can't agree more.

"What does that mean?" I ask him, peering over at him as I drive him back to our house where I plan on stripping him out of his clothes and making him know how much I appreciate what he's doing for our baby. How much I love his body for nourishing and taking care of our baby.

How much I love him.

My husband grins at me. "It means my little sweet cream puff or bun," he says. "I've never thought of it much before—it's a term of endearment in French."

I laugh. "A sweet bun? As in you have a bun in your oven?"

He squeezes my leg. "We both have a bun in my oven. A sweet, cute cream puff that is going to keep us up at night and make us pull out our hair. And be the second-most wonderful being on the planet after Colton." He winks at me. "Tied for most wonderful."

God, I love him so much. I entwine my fingers in his and give them a light squeeze. We drive, contented in the silence.

"Colton is at Lakelan's house," I remind him, waggling my eyebrows. "Do you want to celebrate back at our place before we go pick him up?"

"*Bien sûr que oui!*" he says, and I let out a laugh.

"Is that a yes?"

"You know it is," he tells me in a sultry voice. He looks at the ultrasound again and sighs contentedly. "Our baby is six inches long," he murmurs in wonder. "I've been a pediatrician for years. And I never realized how...*miraculeuse*...this is."

"Everything changes when you have a baby," I tell him honestly. I remember when Jeremiah found out that he was pregnant with Colton. He nested like a mother hen for the entire nine months and made sure that everything was just perfect for our baby.

"Where are you?" Jacques asks me, picking up on the change in my mood.

"I'm just thinking about Jeremiah," I tell him honestly. In the months since we found out that Jacques was pregnant, I've spoken freely about Jeremiah's pregnancy. How his undiagnosed preeclampsia created a complication when he gave birth that we couldn't have stopped.

Admittedly, I've been a little more than overprotective of Jacques. Granted, I'm sure that he loves the attention that I shower on him. On the other hand, I also know that I can drive him nuts if I take it too far.

This isn't one of those times, though.

He squeezes my hand. "*Mon amour*," he tells me, "I promise this will be different. I have no plans to go anywhere. Dr. Loomis will take care of me."

I believe him. Like me, Dr. Loomis, Jacques's obstetrician, lost his omega. I can't think of a better doctor to place my trust in. Still, though, there is that concern that something could happen.

I let out a breath, which eases the tension in my chest, tension that I didn't know was there. "I love you, omega mine."

"*Je t'aime aussi*," he says.

I've realized ever since we got married that he's been more apt to use French around me. I think before, he was overly concerned about coming across as American, doing everything he could to fit in. But since we admitted our feelings for each other, he's come out of his shell a bit and uses French more and more around me and our friends.

In fact, we've spent many of our sexy times with him teaching me new phrases and words. My fantasies and dreams now are no longer spent with just *oui* and *merci*.

No, my fantasies leading to my *petites morts* are much more colorful now.

There's a car parked in front of our house when I pull up. Beside me, I can sense that Jacques stiffens uncomfortably and he sucks in a sharp breath.

"Do you know who that is?" I ask him as I put the car into park.

He shakes his head. "Not exactly. But…" He unbuckles his seatbelt and gets out of the car at the same time the driver of the other car does. Like they were waiting for us.

It's a woman in a smart pantsuit, reminding me oddly of Scully from *The X-Files*. Did something happen?

I can't get out of the car fast enough.

The woman looks at me, her sunglasses flashing with the sunlight and a grim smile tugs at her lips. "You must be Edwin Schneider," she says, and she holds out her hand for me. I recognize her voice, although so much has happened in the past two hours, I have trouble placing it.

I take her proffered hand and give her a firm shake. Or rather, she gives me a firm shake. She seems to be a strong woman.

"I am," I tell her. "Although I don't know who you are."

Jacques stands with his hand on his belly, a frown on his face. I notice that the woman turns back to him and regards him for a long moment before she takes off her sunglasses.

"My name is Silvia Wagner," she says at length. "I'm the immigration officer assigned to Jacques's case, and I've been working on his new filing of paperwork since you got married on Valentine's Day."

Oh, shit. Right. I can place her voice now. I've spoken with her on the phone several times and sent her evidence that Jacques's and my relationship is real.

I'd nearly forgotten that the circumstances under which we got married are completely different to how we're living now. How life has changed.

"Officer Wagner," I say, giving her a smile. "Sorry, we weren't expecting you today."

She snickers. "Well, I was going to do what we call a *bed check*. Show up unannounced to your house to see that you and Dr. Marchand are truly living how your application says you are."

A bed check. Jacques's lawyer has told us about that possibility, but in all the excitement and preparation for our baby, I'd nearly forgotten that as well. Hell, I nearly forgot that Jacques had an ongoing investigation into his ability to stay in America lawfully.

I swallow back the unease in my throat. "You *were* going to do a bed check?" I ask, catching that she had used the past tense when she spoke. "What changed?"

"Well," she says, and she looks Jacques up and down again, as if to double-check that she wasn't being fooled. "It appears that Jacques is pregnant. And that's something that doesn't happen in immigration fraud."

"It doesn't?" Jacques asks sharply, and I almost hiss to him to tell him to stop.

She shakes her head. "Very rarely. Even so, that child you're carrying is an American citizen. There are avenues for you to stay on with that. Where were you two coming home from?"

As if she knows.

"We just came back from our twenty-week checkup," Jacques tells her proudly, holding his head upright. "We had an ultrasound."

She cocks her head, interested. "May I see the ultrasound?" she asks, holding her hand out for it.

I can see Jacques's hesitation, as if letting this immigration see the image of our baby is going to ruin this moment somehow. Finally, sensibility wins out and he hands over the image to her.

She takes it from him and gives it a long look, frowning down at it. I know that it has Jacques's name at the top, and that it has indisputable proof that our child is growing within him. Even if she came here thinking to catch us in a sham marriage, surely this changes everything.

For a long, long moment, she says nothing.

And then she chuckles and shakes her head. "Twenty weeks," she says softly. "I remember my own at twenty weeks. That first ultrasound. And this is your first baby?" she asks us.

She must know the answer to this, but I can't help gushing. "Jacques's first and my second."

She nods again and hands the ultrasound back to Jacques. My husband takes it from her and holds it to his chest, like it's the most precious thing in the world.

She notices this as well, and she looks between us. "Congratulations, daddies," she says, breaking into a wide grin.

"*Merci*," I find myself saying in French, which dispels the tension, and both Officer Wagner and Jacques burst out laughing. Hard. Enough to have them both crying within a few minutes.

That's when I know that everything is going to work out.

"Well," Officer Wagner says, wiping away the tears from her eyes. "I came here, hoping to find evidence that this was all a fraud, but...even after twelve years on this job, I can still be surprised. Congratulations on your beautiful marriage," she tells us. She nods to Jacques's belly. "And congratulations on your baby. I'm sure you two will be bringing him into a loving, sweet home."

"We will," Jacques promises her, and I can tell that he's holding his breath, waiting for the next words out of Officer Wagner's mouth to be the words he's been wishing for this entire time.

To my immense relief, they are.

"When I get back to my office," she says, "I'll push through the approvals on your green card. Despite a few inconsistencies, I can tell that this is a genuine relationship."

Jacques tenses up next to me. "You mean...?"

She nods. "You're approved, Dr. Marchand. As soon as that comes through, you're welcome to stay in America as long as you wish."

The change in Jacques is immediate. He bursts into tears and clings to me as he takes in great, sobbing breaths. I wrap my arms around him and soothe him.

"Everything is fine," I promise him. "You can stay here with me. Everything is fine, omega mine."

Officer Wagner watches us silently and crosses her arms. "There are a lot of downsides to my job," she tells us. "Where I have to turn down applications for those who don't meet requirements or try to play the system. But every so often, there is a happy ending."

A happy ending. That's what this is. And that's what I know it to be. I hold Jacques to me and kiss his forehead.

"Do you hear that, my love?" I tell him. "A happy ending."

All he does is laugh and cry. And honestly, I've never seen him happier.

I've never been happier as well.

"THERE IS SO MUCH conflicting advice about cribs," I mutter as I watch Edwin put together the bassinet for our baby. I stand next to him, putting a hand over the swell of my stomach, feeling our child's foot push against me. "One says to lay babies on their backs. The other says to put them on their stomachs. And…"

"Everything will be fine," Edwin assures me as he sets the bassinet upright for the first time. "This came recommended to me by all of the most famous magazines, and it's what Colton slept in for the first few months of his life."

I shake my head. "I don't know how you did it. You're keeping me sane with this baby. I don't know how you did it alone with Colton."

He gets to his feet and wraps me in his arms, taking the weight of my thirty-six-week pregnant belly off me and I sigh into him, grateful to have the weight off me even for a moment.

"You rise to the occasion," he murmurs in my ear before nibbling at my earlobe. "I had many, many sleepless nights, worrying about Colton. But you do what you have to do. And I know you'll make a great omega-father to our baby."

"Do you wish we found out the sex of the baby first?" I ask him.

He shakes his head. "So much of our lives are already planned and scripted out. Let's keep the magic and the surprise of this going as long as possible." He kisses my forehead. "You're going to be a great father," he tells me again.

I can tell that the notion excites him, that he can wait to share this with me.

Frankly, neither can I.

"So that's it?" I ask, nodding to the bassinet. "It's all ready?"

Edwin nods. "Yep. All that's left is to put the baby in there."

"Well, and to finish off decorating the nursery," I tell him. "We still have to put up the curtains, assemble the rocking chair, sort the stuffed animals, put the mobile together, buy baby monitors, and…"

"Hush, omega mine," Edwin says, and he kisses me deeply. "Everything will be fine."

And, despite my pregnancy brain going at a million kilometers an hour, I truly do believe him. I don't think I could get through all this without him.

"Unicorns!" Colton cries from the doorway. We both turn to see him staring agape at the decorations we've put up in the baby's room. He lets out an excited whoop. "Can I share a room with my baby brother or sister? Please, please, please, please?"

Edwin opens his mouth, then shuts it and looks helplessly at me. I know he has trouble saying no to Colton, and he sometimes worry that he lets his son walk all over him, but in this case…

"Sure you can," I promise him. "Once the baby is old enough to sleep in their own room, okay? Until then, this can be yours." I sweep my hand around the room, and Colton's eyes get even bigger.

"Really?"

I nod. "Really."

He hugs me and then runs out of the room, I assume, to our room to gather his things to move in. I chuckle and shake my head.

Edwin surprises me by wrapping his arms around my middle. "You didn't have to do that, omega mine."

I playfully bat at him. "Whatever do you mean? I'm simply creating a stronger bond between Colton and our unborn baby, *while* opening up our bedroom so that we can have our own playtime whenever we want."

He kisses me deeply. "I always knew you were devious."

I put a hand on my belly. "I have to be to keep up with you and Colton. And our baby-to-be."

He takes my hand. "Come with me, omega mine. And I'll show you just how devious I can be."

———

I'VE HEARD of that old saying that you're not supposed to have sex in the final days of your pregnancy. That a good orgasm can trigger labor and all the plans you have can go out the window.

That's what happens to me that night.

I wake up with a gasp, clutching at my spasming belly. I've been plagued with Braxton-Hicks contractions my entire third trimester, making for a few scary moments, but there's something about this that feels different.

Like it's time.

Before waking Edwin up, I wait to see if it's another contraction or if it's just a crazy dream that I had. A part of me wishes it were. I'm not ready yet. The nursery isn't ready and there are so many things I want to do before the baby comes.

But another contraction does come, and this time, it does make me cry out.

"*Merde!*"

Edwin's awake in a flash. "Jacques?" He puts a hand on my shoulder. "Jacques, what is it, love?"

"The baby," I say through gritted teeth. "Remember how they said not to have sex too close to my due date?"

Even in the pale moonlight, Edwin pales. "The baby is coming?"

I nod. "I think so."

He's on his feet in a flash, grabbing our hospital bag and running to the nursery where Colton is sleeping. Meanwhile, I manage to amble to my feet and waddle to the closet to get a bathrobe on when I feel water dripping down my legs.

"My water broke!" I shout to Edwin. I've prepared for this moment for nine months, if not my whole life, and yet I still feel woefully unprepared

Luckily, he's at my side again, taking me by the elbow while he carries a sleeping Colton with one arm. "I've called Slade and Zach," he says, bringing up Colton's best friend Lakelan's parents. "They're going to meet us at the hospital to take care of Colton."

All a part of our birth plan, but it still feels like everything is happening too fast.

We get down to the car, and Edwin buckles Colton into his car seat and helps me in.

"Hurry," I hiss through gritted teeth as he runs around to the driver's side of the car.

Thankfully, Edwin does. He takes my hand, squeezes it, puts the car in reverse and drives. "You're doing beautifully, omega mine," he whispers.

I'm not sure about that.

We get to Vale Valley General Hospital, where Dr. Loomis is already there, waiting for us with a wheelchair. He's grinning, apparently in a much more jovial mood than I feel.

"Looks like it's baby time, Jacques," he says to me in a way too cheerful voice.

I respond by cursing at him in a way that makes me glad that Colton is asleep and doesn't understand French too well at this point. Dr. Loomis, for his part, laughs and takes us into the delivery room where I change into a hospital gown and propped up on the chair. Edwin gets dressed in scrubs, and he has a camera, capturing the whole scene ahead of us.

How is he so calm? Everything is going to shit, and he's grinning like a crazy man.

I curse at him too, and he chuckles.

"I blame you for this," I mutter.

He kisses my forehead and smoothes back my hair. "I'm thankful to you for this, *mon mari*," he counters. At hearing myself be called his "mon mari," I burst into tears.

What transpires is an agonizing eight hours of waiting for the contractions to get closer together. Eight hours of Edwin holding my hand and telling me that everything will be all right, even though he knows firsthand just how badly things can go wrong.

I love him for it. I love every damn piece of him for this.

And when Dr. Loomis finally decides that it's time for me to push, he's holding onto my hand and doing double duty, alternating between getting everything on camera and supporting me.

"Push, Jacques," Dr. Loomis chant. "Push, *si vouz plait!*"

Not the French I would use, but I utilize my irritation to push harder and harder until...

A baby's cry cuts through the tension of the delivery room, and I start sobbing in exhaustion.

"It's a boy!" Dr. Loomis cries, as he holds up my son for me to see.

I start crying real tears now, because I've never seen anything so beautiful. Edwin is crying as well and he holds me as we both marvel at my son together.

"What are you going to name him?" one of the nurses asks.

Edwin and I have been planning on names. We had everything planned, but seeing my son now, I know that we don't have anything appropriate.

Not like this.

"Valentine," I say. "After the day his papa and I got married."

Edwin gives me a shocked look, but then chuckles before kissing me deeply. He places a big hand on the baby's head and looks down at our son, almost in disbelief.

"Valentine it is."

EPILOGUE

JACQUES

PEOPLE USED to notice my French accent when they first meet me.

Now they notice my son before anything else. And I love every moment of it.

"Oh my goodness!" a woman on the bus exclaims. "Your baby is adorable! How old is he?"

I look up to see the kindly old woman from a long time ago, the one that I had talked to on my way into the hospital one day. I haven't seen her since then, and just reflecting on how much has changed in my life since then, I smile.

Because back then, I simply lived in Vale Valley. Now it's my home. And I know that for certain more than anything in my life.

"Just four months old," I tell her, and I bounce little Valentine in his baby carrier. "He's a spry little guy."

Now I think my accent has given me away, because her face breaks into a wide smile. "Oh, my goodness! It's you! How are you doing?"

"*Merveilleusement,*" I say, unable to hide my returning grin. "Life can just be *magnifique* in all the right ways."

She nods and crosses her arms. "Well, you have a beautiful son," she says.

Beautiful and absolutely perfect, just like my Edwin and Colton. And as I get off the bus to greet my little family waiting for me at the bus stop by my house, I know that I'm in the right place. Life can be strange and scary, but with the right people, it's entirely worth it.

Especially seeing Edwin's smile. He kisses the top of Valentine's head before kissing me and whispering into my ear, "Omega, *je t'aime.*"

WANT MORE FROM SUMMER CHASE? **Here's sneak peak of The Back-Up Date, her other Vale Valley Valentine book co-written with Trisha Linde, available for free in Kindle Unlimited.**

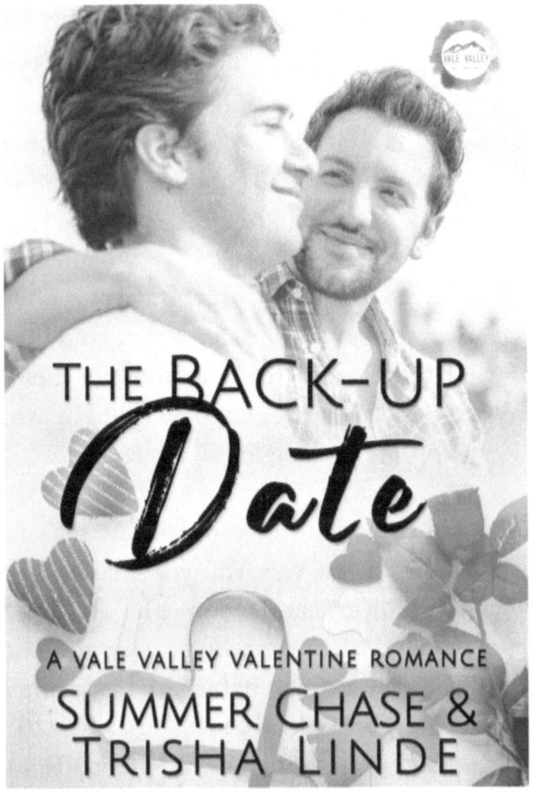

**Roses are red. Danny feels blue.
This Valentine's, his friend Nate
Makes all his dreams come true!**

Best friends for life…

Alpha Nate has known Omega Danny his whole life, yet he never tried anything beyond that for fear of losing his best friend. But with Danny being interested in this guy he met online, Nate realizes that he may lose his chance to find out if there's anything more.

...turn into lovers...

When Danny sets up a date for Valentine's Day with Kevin, the hot alpha he met online, he never expected to be stood up. Or that rejection would hurt so much. Luckily, his best friend Nate is there to comfort him. In more ways than one.

...with a baby on the way!

Then Danny finds out that he's pregnant, and these best friends will have to see if there's a future for them. And they may just find that a back-up date could be what they were looking for all along.

The Back-Up Date features in the second season of the multi-author series about Vale Valley, a small town open to everyone in need of love and a home. It's an MM Mpreg romance perfect for readers who love friends to lovers stories, male pregnancy, cute babies, and amazing HEAs. Pull up a chair, grab a box of chocolates, and settle in for this smexy and sweet standalone Valentine's Romance read!

Get it here

READ ON FOR AN EXCERPT...

"WHY NOT ASK HIM OUT?" Danny asked, pointing with his beer bottle toward the bar. I followed his gaze to see a muscular, strong omega leaning against the counter. I noticed that he was staring back at us, and our eyes connected for the briefest moment before I ducked back into my pint of beer.

"Not my type," I muttered before covering up my embarrassment with swig of Guinness. "Besides, I think he just wants free drinks tonight."

"And who wouldn't?" Danny asked. He elbowed me in the ribs. "Free drinks *and* he'd get to talk to you. Plus," he added, giving me a devilish grin, "it could put you in the running for a date for Valentine's Day."

As much as I hated to admit it, Valentine's Day was a week away, and I was, yet again, not in a relationship with someone to spend it with. I'd just had a nasty breakup with my ex Braidon back in September and hadn't really felt the inclination to jump into a relationship with anyone else.

Then again, it could have been the omega sitting across from me. But Danny was untouchable, someone that I shouldn't have feelings for. I would have rather had Danny as my best friend than ruin it with romantic feelings.

Because I'd learned a long time ago that I had terrible luck when it came to love.

So I just sat back and frowned into my drink. "No, thanks. I'll have a date with Sylvester Stallone." Danny raised a confused eyebrow, and I rolled my eyes before playfully flicking his nose. "Rocky movies, Danny. I'm going to get drunk and watch Rocky."

"What? Why?" He sounded so scandalized by my Valentine's plans or lack thereof.

"Because Valentine's was a holiday made up by the greeting card and chocolate companies to guilt people into feeling like they had to take out their significant others and buy them shit they don't need."

"That's not true," Danny protested.

"Really? Prove it?"

He pulled out his phone and thumbed in a search. "Here!" he cried, triumphant. He settled in closer to me, reading his screen as he did so. "In the 3rd century A.D., the Roman Emperor Claudius II executed two men — both named Valentine — on Feb. 14, giving them martyrdom that was then celebrated by the Catholic Church as Saint Valentine." His face fell as he read it and I couldn't help my snicker.

"Doesn't sound too romantic, does it?" I nudged him back with my shoulder.

"Well, Valentine's is what you make of it," he said defensively.

"And I'm going to make it a date between me, my couch, and Rocky Balboa," I said.

Danny groaned. "Why don't you at least make an effort to find a date for Valentine's? You're a good-looking man, Nate. And you're smart, funny, and--"

"Stop, you're embarrassing me." I said it good-naturedly, however I truly was starting to feel embarrassed by his words. Especially since they were coming from him. After all, I was trying so damn hard to ignore these feelings for him.

I wanted to protect him. To make sure that no one would break his heart.

It was a feeling that some people felt for their best friends. However, I had the notion that most people weren't in love with their best friends and that drove their overprotectiveness.

I needed a damn hobby or something.

"You shouldn't be embarrassed," Danny said, oblivious to my scowl. "You need to go out there. Find someone. Make cute babies that creepily look like you. And live happily ever after."

I really, really wanted him to stop, because all I could imagine as he said that was a life with him. God, I was screwed if I didn't get my head out of my ass and moved on from crushing on him hard.

I opened my mouth to say something--what I wasn't sure, because he jumped as his phone beeped.

"Oh," he said with a grin. "It's Kevin!"

I raised an eyebrow, at his genuine delight as he started texting the alpha back. At least, I thought he was an alpha. Danny had started talking to this guy through a dating app, and they'd been chatting up nonstop ever since.

Something inside my chest twisted at the thought that some other alpha was making Danny happy instead of me. But I couldn't deny the happiness that showed on my best friend's face as he texted this guy back.

Danny really liked him. At least for his texting skills. He hadn't met him yet, so I consoled myself with the thought that they might never meet and perhaps I could go in and sweep Danny off his feet.

If I could ever get the balls to approach Danny like someone beyond my friend.

Danny chuckled to himself and pocketed the phone.

"What did he say?" I asked, leaning forward on my elbows.

"Oh, he's just telling me about the latest show at the Vale Valley Repertory Theatre," he said. "There are two dragon shifters there who can apparently act better than Sylvester Stallone."

I smirked. "You take that back."

He shook his head. "Nuh-uh." But he kept grinning.

I licked my lips, unable to keep my thoughts to myself any longer. "So when is Text-And-Talk Kevin going to turn into Meet-In-Person Kevin?"

Danny looked contemplative for a moment before sighing and shrugging. "Not sure. I keep waiting for him to ask me out, but he hasn't."

"And you're not going to ask him out?" For a moment, I had a flutter of hope that maybe this flirtation between him and Kevin would die before they ever met.

"Well," he said, thinking about it. "You think I could ask him?"

Shit. "Uh, maybe?" That wasn't how it was supposed to go down at all.

He looked at me for a long moment, and I couldn't read his expression. Contemplative? Or waiting for me to step in and tell him my feelings? Or maybe…

But before my mind could go down that road, he finally nodded. "You're right, of course. I should ask him out. I'm a handsome, strong omega. I don't have to wait for an alpha to ask me out." He patted my hand. "You're a good friend, Nate."

Shit and hell and damnation.

I managed a smile. "I have to be a good friend to keep up with you." A spineless, stupid answer, when all I wanted to do was tell him how I felt. But no, I went for the Switzerland route and remained neutral throughout all of this.

Dammit. Fuck.

Danny watched me for a long moment before nodding. "I'll ask him tomorrow." He chuckled. "I've had one too many beers, so I may make a fool out of myself." He combed a hand through his hair. Hair that I'd imagined running my own hands through.

I was a certifiable idiot.

"Speaking of one too many beers," he said with a

groan as he pushed his chair back, "I need to go to the little boy's room."

He got up from his seat and ambled his way over to the back of the bar where the restrooms were. I watched him for a long moment, wondering what else I could have said to turn this all around and then berated myself for thinking that way.

Danny was my best friend. I didn't want to fuck up the best friend a guy could have.

A hand slapped on the table, and the omega from the bar grinned down at me in a way that he must have thought was sultry. "How about you buy me a beer, alpha?"

He was ballsy, I had to give him that. Especially since I'd been sitting here with another omega, but maybe it was painfully obvious to everyone around me that we were just friends. Or maybe it was that this guy didn't care.

"Nah," I said, taking another sip out of my Guinness. "Not interested."

And that was the absolute truth.

The omega had the gall to look offended before storming off to find some other alpha to harrass for free drinks.

I sighed and leaned back in my chair.

Why the hell was I so preoccupied with Danny? I should have just been keeping him at the distance I'd always kept him. Safe in the friendzone.

Because otherwise, we'd end up breaking both of our hearts. I wasn't sure if our friendship would survive that.

So in the friendzone I'd remain.

Which meant it was going to be another shitty Valentine's Day alone.

ABOUT THE AUTHOR

Summer Chase loves naughty boys, and she loves them even more when they turn out to be nice guys, too. She's the pen name for a New York Times bestselling author who wanted to have another name like a superhero.

You can keep up with all her latest releases by signing up to her newsletter here: http://eepurl.com/dPCqLb

Vale Valley Season 2 Book 8
    A Hatchling for Valentine's by M.M. Wilde

Vale Valley Season 2 Book 9
    Omega, je t'aime by Summer Chase

Vale Valley Season 2 Book 10
    Renewed Faith by Michael Mandrake

Vale Valley Season 2 Book 11
    The Back-Up Date by Summer Chase and Trisha Linde

Vale Valley Season 2 Book 12
    Bewitching Love by Giovanna Reaves

www.ingramcontent.com/pod-product-compliance
Lightning Source LLC
Chambersburg PA
CBHW031321060726
47590CB00003B/1293